DISNEY'S
My Very First Winnie the Pooh™

Roo's Messy Room

Written by
Betty Birney

Illustrated by
Nancy Stevenson

SCHOLASTIC INC.

New York Toronto London Auckland Sydney
Mexico City New Delhi Hong Kong Buenos Aires

Published by Scholastic Inc., 90 Old Sherman Turnpike, Danbury, CT 06816
by arrangement with Disney Licensed Publishing.

SCHOLASTIC and associated logos are trademarks
and/or registered trademarks of Scholastic Inc.

ISBN 0-7172-8904-4

Printed in the U.S.A.

"What a mess!" Kanga said, looking at Roo's room. "Please tidy it up."

"But, Mama," Roo replied, "every time I clean my room, it just gets messy again. Besides, it doesn't bother me."

"Well, it bothers me," said Kanga. "I can't even get to your dresser!"

Then Kanga got an idea about how to teach Roo a lesson.

"I've decided you're right," Kanga told Roo. "I don't think you should clean your room if you don't want to. After all, it will just get dirty again."

"Great!" Roo cried. "Tigger and Pooh are coming over to play."

Roo was soon joined by his friends.

"Oh, bother!" Pooh complained. "It's raining. We can't play outside."

"That's okay. We'll play in my room," Roo replied. "It's already messy."

"Hoo-hoo-hoo!" cried Tigger, bouncing gleefully. "Tiggers just love messy rooms!"

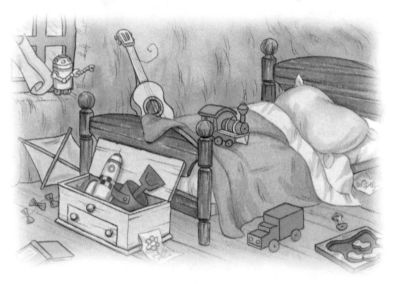

Pooh, Tigger, and
Roo had a great time.
They threw papers on
the floor and tossed
toys and games
everywhere. It was
fun for a while, until
there was no more
room to play in all
the mess.

Then Roo got an idea. He put on his raincoat and picked up his pail.

"Where are you going?" Kanga asked Roo.

"To get some mud," Roo answered excitedly. "We're going to make mud pies!"

Kanga was upset to hear this, but she stuck to her plan.

"It's your room," Kanga said. "You can do whatever you want."

Roo returned with the mud. He and his friends made lots of mud pies. And Roo's room got messier and messier and messier.

"Oh, bother!" Pooh said after a while. "Things are sticking to me!"

"Ouch and double ouch!" yelled Tigger, as he stepped on a toy. "There's no room to bounce comfortably! Tiggers hate messy rooms!"

As soon
as it stopped
raining, Tigger and Pooh
said good-bye. Roo got lonely, so he packed up
some toys and set off to find someone
to play with.

"Dear me, Roo!" Owl called
after him. "You're littering up
the Hundred-Acre Wood."
"Oops, sorry!"
said Roo.

Soon Roo came to Piglet's house.

"Hi, Piglet," Roo said. "May I come in and play?"

"Well, I just cleaned my house, Roo," Piglet replied. "You *may* come in if you promise not to make a mess."

"Yes, I promise," said Roo.

Roo wiped his muddy hands and feet and left his wagon outside. Inside, Pooh and Tigger were happily playing.

"Howdy-do, Roo!" Tigger yelled. "Isn't Piglet's place Tiggerific? You can bounce without stepping on stuff!"

Roo nodded. It surely was. All of Piglet's games and puzzles and art supplies were neatly labeled and kept in a special place.

Soon Roo was also having a wonderful time playing in Piglet's tidy house.

"Golly! I can find anything I want," Roo said. "We could play here forever!"

"Yes," Pooh agreed. "If only Piglet had more pots of honey."

Roo was having so much fun, he lost track of time.

"I've been looking all over for you, Roo," Kanga said, arriving at Piglet's house. "It's time for dinner."

"He'll be right with you, Kanga," said Pooh. "Piglet has a rule that all his friends must help put his toys away before they leave."

That night Roo had a problem. It was bedtime, but he couldn't find his bed in all the mess!

"Well, you can either try to find your bed, or sleep on the couch tonight," Kanga kindly suggested. "It's your decision, dear."

The next morning, Piglet told Pooh and Tigger about an idea he had. Then they went to visit Roo. They were carrying boxes.

"Hiya, buddy boy!" Tigger said to Roo. "We're here to have a tee-rific party!"

"Sorry, guys," Roo said sadly, "but my room is too messy for a party."

"Well, that's just right," chuckled Pooh, "because this is a cleaning-up party!"

With his friends' help, Roo soon had a clean room. All of his things were in their own special places. It would be easy to keep his room neat from now on.

"It looks great!" said Roo excitedly.

"Hoo-hoo-hoo, it do!" Tigger cried. "And if you put your things away when you're finished playing with them, there's much more room for bouncing, see?"

They celebrated with a picnic outside.

"I'm so proud of you, Roo dear," Kanga said. "You cleaned your room, and I didn't even have to ask you."

"Now I'll keep everything clean!" Roo said.

"Me, too," Pooh added. "See? I've already cleaned my plate! Um, may I please have another smackerel of honey?"